Harcourt, Inc.

Orlando Austin New York San Diego London

Jack the Tripper

GENE BARRETTA

POLLY was the first student at Benjamin Dizzie Elementary to go down. "I got tripped!" she cried as she stumbled into the classroom.

"I was minding my own business," Polly continued, "just thinking about my book report—my *extra long* book report—when out of nowhere, there he was!"

Whooooooo

Everyone gasped.

"All I saw was a black top hat and cape." Polly shivered. "He grabbed my *extra long, extra wonderful* book report and ran."

Mrs. Fletcher tried to calm her. "Oh, don't worry about your book report, dear. You must be terribly shaken."

ooosh!

In fact, the whole class was shaken, and a bit stirred. But they were smiling by photo time. After all, the annual Dizzie Day Parade was only four days away. Dizzie costumes! Dizzie candy! Dizzie dancing! The parade was a strange one, but then so was the school's founder, Dr. Dizzie.

Yes, he was wise. Sure, he was noble. Yet he combed his hair with a fork and his best friend was a monkey. Every year he led the Dizzie Day Parade with the bold command, "**Anything Goes!**"

The children worked hard to finish their parade costumes.

Suddenly, Winston burst through the door. "I got tripped!" he shouted. He dropped an empty candy box onto his desk. "The tripper is still out there. And now he's eating our parade candy!"

"My goodness, you poor boy," said Mrs. Fletcher. "Well, we can always get more candy. The important thing is that you're safe."

But the tripper struck again.

"He said his name was Jack," Catherine sobbed.

"Jack the Tripper," added Mary. "Mommy, I want to go home."

The next day was no better.

"I got tripped," said Reggie.

"He got us both with one boot!" claimed the twins.

The headmaster offered the children toys and sweets. He even replaced their torn clothes. "Jack the Tripper must be stopped," he declared.

The whole town was tense and jittery. Parents rushed to the school and demanded answers. They searched every cranny, nook, and crack for clues.

Still, it was Dizzie Day, and the children arrived at school in their costumes chanting, "Anything Goes! Anything Goes!"

But instead, everything stopped.

Dr. Dizzie made a devastating announcement. "I'm afraid there can be no parade," he said. "Not when Jack the Tripper is lurking."

The students' jaws dropped. Their eyes popped.

"Wait!" Polly jumped to her feet. "Please don't cancel the parade! I . . . I . . . I . . ."

"What is it, dear?" asked Mrs. Fletcher.

"I lied!" said Polly. "There is no Jack. And I never wrote that book report. It's true, I did trip . . ."

"But I was alone."

And then Reggie stood up. "Please don't cancel the parade. I lied, too. You treated Polly so well . . . I figured, why not?"

"We lied to get our names in the paper," the twins admitted.

Catherine and Mary chimed in. "We lied because it worked for Winston."

Winston's confession was short and sweet.

"Burp."

Every child had something to add. Dr. Dizzie and Mrs. Fletcher were shocked!

The only parade Dr. Dizzie would lead that day
was out of the classroom and down the hall.

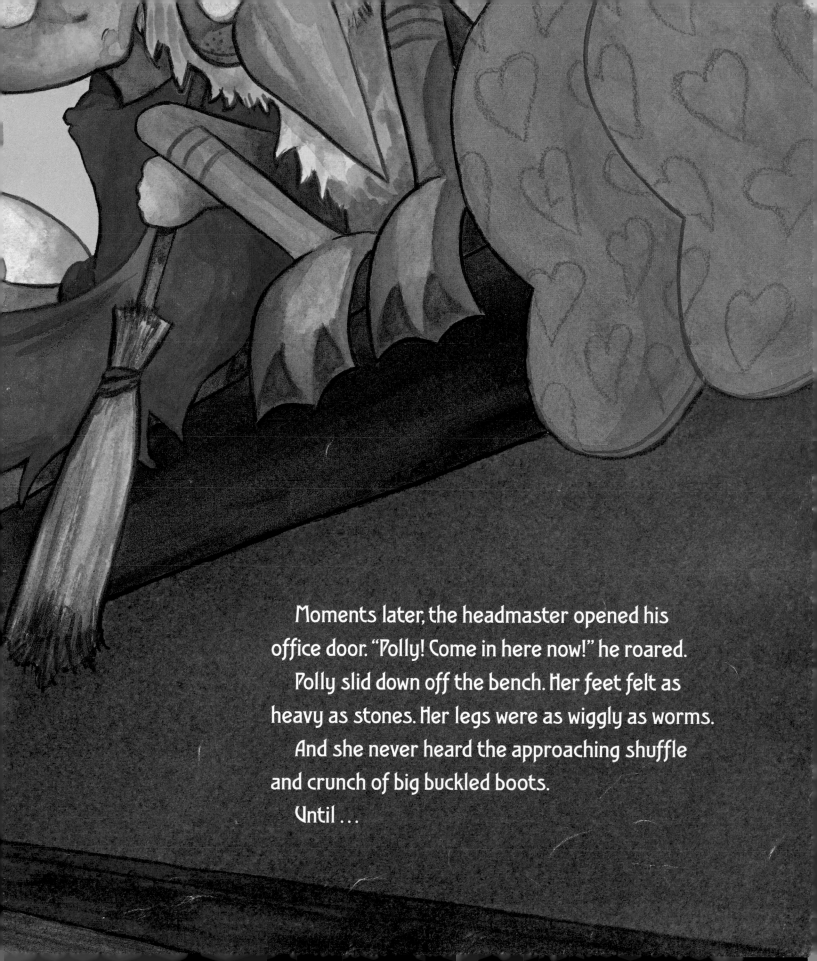

Moments later, the headmaster opened his office door. "Polly! Come in here now!" he roared.

Polly slid down off the bench. Her feet felt as heavy as stones. Her legs were as wiggly as worms.

And she never heard the approaching shuffle and crunch of big buckled boots.

Until . . .

Everyone screamed and scattered.

A dark figure leaped forward.
"Let me know when you finish that
book report, Polly. I'd love to read it."
Then he was gone.

The headmaster stepped into the hall.
The children circled him shouting, "Jack the
Tripper's here! Jack the Tripper's here!"
   But the headmaster just shook his head.
"Yes, and a horse has five legs. Enough of this
nonsense. Polly, get up off the floor."

Was it Jack? It looked like him,
judging by the clothes.
Yet as he ran, how strange it was . . .
that he called out,

"Anything Goes!"

www.HarcourtBooks.com

Library of Congress Cataloging-in-Publication Data
Barretta, Gene.
Jack the Tripper/Gene Barretta.
p. cm.
Summary: Someone is tripping students at Benjamin Dizzie Elementary School and
taking their candy and homework, but the resulting nervousness does not quell people's
excitement over the upcoming Dizzie Day Parade, where the rule is "anything goes."
[1. Elementary schools—Fiction. 2. Schools—Fiction. 3. Honesty—Fiction.
4. Eccentrics and eccentricities—Fiction.] I. Title.
PZ7.B275366Jac 2008
[E]—dc22   2007033421
ISBN 978-0-15-206132-6

First edition
H G F E D C B A

Manufactured in China

The illustrations in this book were done in watercolors on Arches cold press paper.
The display type was created by Tom Seibert.
The text type was set in Quaint Gothic.
Color separations by SC Graphic Technology Pte Ltd, Singapore
Manufactured by South China Printing Company, Ltd., China
Production supervision by Christine Witnik
Designed by April Ward

For Ben Chatrer—clippity-cloppity
horse feet and a man's haircut.
And for Benjamin Goldberg—
Ceci n'est pas un livre.

Special thanks to Donald Rumbelow
for his great walking tour.